Addict 3.0
DeAngelo's Story

By Porsha Deun

Books by Porsha Deun

<u>The Love Lost Series</u>
Love Lost
Love Lost Forever
Love Lost Revenge

<u>The Addict Series</u>
Addict – A Fatal Attraction Story
Addict 2.0 – Andre's Story
Addict 3.0 – DeAngelo's Story
Addict – DeMario's Story (August 2021)

<u>Standalones</u>
Intoxic (Oct 2021)

<u>Children's Book</u>
Princesses Can Do Anything!

ADDICT 3.0 – DEANGELO'S STORY. Copyright © 2021 by Porsha Deun. All rights reserved. Printed in the United States of America for Porsha Deun, LLC. For information, email Porsha Deun, porshadeun@gmail.com.

All characters, places, and events are fiction and not real. Any likeness is a coincidence and not intentional.

All rights reserved. No parts of this book may be reproduced by any mechanical, photographic, or electronic process, or in the form of a phonographic recording; nor may it be stored in a retrieval system, transmitted, or otherwise copied for public or private use – other than for "fair use" as brief quotations embodied in articles and reviews – without prior written permission of the author.

ISBN (paperback)

Library of Congress Control Number:

To my bestfriend Tamika,

You are truly one of the best people I know. I love and admire you greatly.

Addict 3.0
DeAngelo's Story

By Porsha Deun

Chapter 1

I was in court every single day of my brother's murder trial. I shouldn't have been shocked at seeing Andre there supporting the murderer, but I was, given her actions and how she used him to make it seem like she had moved on. Yeah, I stopped saying her name. She was nothing more to me than the crazy hoe that took my brother, my best friend since we were conceived, away from me and everyone who loved him.

Back to Andre. I knew he was in love with the hoe from the moment I met him. I told him she would do him wrong. Only then, I didn't know her wrong would have a permanent ripple effect on my life, too. Andre was in deep still after all she did.

I didn't understand that shit, so I confronted Andre about it after the second day in court. He was standing on the steps outside the courthouse. "Why are you sticking by her?" I yelled at him as I approached.

"She needs support. I'm always going to stand by her."

"She murdered my brother."

"Who lied to her, nearly choked her to death, and used her like she was a sex toy, the same as you."

My fist connected with his face before I realized my arm was moving. Andre stumbled down the rest of the steps and I was hot on his tail. "Don't put this on my brother!" I yelled as I chased after him. I didn't give a damn that he was bigger than me. I could hold my own and that day, in that moment, I was going to beat his ass for what he said...and for being a dumbass.

He surprised me with a hard punch of his own when I got within reach of him. "I love her! You and your brother just used her. Took advantage of her sex drive." I swung at him, but he dodged and hit me in the side. "Be mad at yourself because you were the one that brought your brother to Destiny."

Those words punched me in the gut and stopped me in my tracks.

"Stop! Stop it!" It was Kim's voice, but I couldn't turn my eyes from Andre. Her heels came clicking and clacking down the steps until she was standing between us on the sidewalk. "Stop it. DeAngelo, this won't bring DeMario back."

It would make me feel good though.

I didn't tell her that. Plus, I wasn't ready for Kim to find out I was the one who introduced DeMario to the person who would later become his murderer. She asked after the hoe showed her the video of me walking in for the last group session we had. All of that would come out in court.

"Take me home," she requested.

"I'm not done with him yet," I said.

"Nothing you say or do to him will change what has already happened, nor will it change what he thinks or feels for Destiny," Kim stated. I growled at the mention of her name. "DeAngelo, take me home."

I was starting to regret that I offered to be her ride back and forth to court for the duration of the trial, but it was the only way to get out of being in the car with other family members. Most of them blamed Kim for falling for the murderer's set up. They had no idea how convincing and manipulating the murderer could be when she wanted to. Plus, my family didn't know the extent of my involvement with the hoe, also something else that would come out in court. I was already distancing myself from them because I knew some would cut me off once they found out. I had changed the locks on my condo in anticipation that a couple of my cousins would somehow get hold to copies of my keys and try to set me up after I took the stand a day or two later.

I pointed two fingers at Andre's dumbass. "You are a fucking fool. I'm gonna show you how much of a fool you are if you come at me again." I spat at his feet to punctuate my point. "Let's go, Kim!"

She jumped at my snap but recovered quickly and followed me down the sidewalk to the Broad Street parking lot. We got into my black Charger Hellcat without another word until we were about to exit the parking lot. Kim was holding money out to me. I looked at her like she was crazy. I may have fucked women like I had no respect for them, but I was raised with some manners.

"No," I told her.

"I told you I would pay for parking if you let me ride with you. This is me keeping my word." She paused. "It's the least I can do."

I released a heavy sigh before taking the bills from her to pay the fare. Pulling out the parking lot, I headed to Claiborne Avenue to get on HWY 90 WEST. My mind was in a number of places as I headed towards the port on the way to Kim's place. I wasn't looking forward to seeing my mother's face once I put everything out in court. I also wondered how fucked up and unorganized the kitchen would be at the restaurant I'm head chef at, though, I was grateful the manager told me to take as much time off as I needed for the trial.

Then there was that crazy ass Andre. Something told me to leave him and that broad alone after our first threesome. I knew then that she was crazy, and he was crazy in love with her. Over time each of their respective editions of crazy grew. I hoped I didn't have to worry about Andre moving forward. I wanted to be done with this mess as soon as she was sentenced and not have him or anyone else coming after me because of her.

"Do you mind stopping at the market before you take me home?" Kim asked, taking me away from my thoughts.

"Sure." I got off Terry Parkway and make the few turns to the Hong Kong Food Market on Behrman Hwy.

Addict 3.0 – DeAngelo's Story

"You need anything?" she asked.

"Naw. I'm good." I let her out in front of the building between the two dragon statues on either side of the door. The dragons look like the one the little red dragon broke in the cartoon movie about the girl who took her father's place in the imperial army I used to watch with my brothers and sister when we were kids. The market sat in the middle of Gretna, one of the many suburbs of New Orleans, in the Jefferson Parish. It's changed some since Katrina, like much of the area.

My car announced I was getting a call. Good thing my phone connected to the car automatically because in the shit with Andre, I forgot to check it when I got in the car. I just wanted to get as far away from him and Destiny as soon as possible.

"Tiana," I answered.

"Hey sexy. Are you busy?" That was Tiana's way of asking if I wanted to come through to fuck.

"I'll be free in about twenty, thirty minutes. What you cook?"

"I got some ox tails, red beans and rice, collard greens, and cornbread leftovers from yesterday."

"Make me a plate."

"It'll be ready when you get here."

"Alright." With that, I hung up.

Tiana was one of those slim-thick females, like the singer Ashanti. She was light-skinned and pretty like her too. She loved to call me when her kids were away with their father or her mom just as much as she loved to cook. We met at one of those Taste of New Orleans cookoffs and have been messing around ever since. That was a few months before the murderer took my twin brother from me. *Fuck that bitch. The murderer, not Tiana.*

Not long after I hung up with Tiana, Kim was back outside and I pulled out from the parking spot I was in and picked her up, then dropped her off at her place in the Garden Estates.

Done with Kim for the day, I was back on HWY 90 headed towards the lively neighborhood called Central City.

Chapter 2

I stepped into Tiana's place with an 8-pack of beer. She closed the door behind me while wearing nothing but a tank top and some boy shorts that hugged her thick and round ass cheeks perfectly. "Make yourself comfortable. Your plate just finished warming up."

Sitting down on the couch, I immediately opened a beer and took a long swig. Tiana came out the kitchen with a plate of food while sipping from a wine glass. After handing me the plate, she sat next to me and looked me up and down.

"How was court today?"

"I don't want to talk about it," I said before putting a fork full of food in my mouth. I came over here to get away from court, the murderer, and the idiot in love with said murderer. They were the last thing I wanted on my mind right now.

I picked up her remote control and changed the television to a sports news channel. The Saints barely won their game yesterday and they're discussing if Brees should give it up at the end of the season. I kept eating and listening to the sport analysts while Tiana rubbed my neck and the back of my head. Once I was done with the food, I rinsed it all down with beer. Tiana took my plate to the kitchen and when she returned, she kneeled in front of me. Without a word, Tiana undid my pants while I kept drinking my beer and looking at the television. I didn't act completely oblivious to what Tiana was trying to do because I wanted it too, so I lifted myself up off the couch when she tried to pull my pants down.

Tiana sucked on my dick to make it come alive. I finished the beer and tilted my head back, closing my eyes to focus on the beautiful sounds her mouth was making. My hands went into her hair and I guided her to go further down on my dick.

This was exactly what I needed.

My phone rung but I ignored it. Whoever it was could wait. This right here was selfcare for me.

As Tiana went to town on my dick, my phone kept ringing. There was only one person in the world who would ever blow my phone up like that and I was in no place mentally, emotionally, or physically to deal with my mother at the moment. Without looking at my phone, I turned it off and made a mental note to return the calls after I left Tiana's.

I shut out everything that was outside of Tiana's apartment. More importantly, outside of her mouth. The sound of the sports analysts faded the more I focused on her slurps, gulps, and gags. I started rotating my hips to help her find the rhythm I wanted.

Damn, her mouth felt good.

I let the pleasure surround me and got lost in it. It wasn't long before both my hands were in her hair and I was rotating my hips in larger movements. Tiana pulled her head back a little every time I thrusted up, but I didn't want her to run. I wanted my dick in her throat, not near it. My grip in her hair tightened, then in one smooth motion, I flipped over on one hip, forcing her body to flip over with me. Now her back was against the bottom of the couch with the back of her head resting on the cushion. I was bent over her with my dick still in her mouth. Keeping my hands on either side of her head, I fucked her mouth with long, powerful strokes.

Tiana was not the best at deep throating, no matter how much she tried, but in that moment I didn't care. I thrusted my dick into the back of her mouth and then pushed into her throat. Tiana put her hands on my groin to keep me from going as deep as I wanted. I pulled out and looked down at her.

"Move your fucking hands," I growled. "You're always talking about how you want to become a deep throat pro, then come the fuck on."

Tiana moved her hands down my legs. I shook my head.

"Put your hands behind your back." I put the head of my dick on her thick lips. "Keep them there," I instructed. Pushing my dick into the back of her mouth, Tiana began a fight with her gag reflex. Her battle gave me the opening I needed to get into her throat. I slid in and thrusted back and forth.

After a few strokes, Tiana was digging her nails into my calves. She didn't know it at the time, but she earned herself a ten-strike spanking for moving her hands. I decided to give it to her after we fucked. I pulled out of her mouth to let her breathe for a moment and looked down at her.

The face I saw sent a chill through my body and my dick instantly went limp. I was more than confused as to how this happened. It was the face of that murderous slut, but the body didn't match. Also, she was in a cement cell at Orleans Parish Prison. I staggered away from the image in front of me in shock and disgust.

"DeAngelo?" Her face was still there, but now the voice was wrong just like the body was. I didn't understand what was happening to me. I hadn't had a sexual thought about the murderer since the night she killed DeMario. "DeAngelo," she said again.

"Get away from me, you bitch!"

"What the hell is wrong with you?"

The face before me started to morph as the voice registered more with my brain. Tiana's face came into focus, now matching the body in front of me.

"Tiana?"

"You're in my apartment, DeAngelo. Who else would I be?"

"I'm sorry." Embarrassed and confused, I grabbed my underwear and pants, and started putting them on in a haste.

"What just happened to you?"

"I... I don't know."

"Where are you going?" she asked when she realized I was gathering my keys and the rest of the beer.

"I need to get out of here." The words rushed out of my mouth more forcefully than I intended.

"So, you're going to freak out on me and leave me horny?"

"Call one of the dudes in your phone. I gotta go...for both of our good." I walked out of her apartment door before she could say another word. In my car, I rubbed my face and hair as I tried to get control of myself. I was physically shaking from fear that I was losing my mind. I looked at myself in the rearview mirror. "Don't lose it like this. Not over her."

A voice popped up in my head, one I've been fighting off for months.

This is all your fault.

I laid my head on the steering wheel. "Leave me alone."

Not until you admit that this is all your fault.

"You have your blame in your demise too, little brother."

You're older than me by two minutes, so save that little brother shit.

I sighed. "You are dead, Mari. Can't you do like dead folks and rest in peace?"

How can I do that when you haven't made peace with my death, with her, or with yourself?

"I don't have anything to do with her anymore."

That's only because you can't fuck her to death.

"Leave me alone!"

Say her name.

"Leave me be, I said!" I threw my hands against the steering wheel as if I was pushing my brother when he refused to lay off of me.

Say her name.

"Leave! Me! Alone!"

At least admit that you cared for her beyond the sex.

"Shut up!" I screamed at the top of my lungs. With my head still on the steering wheel, I took deep breaths until I felt calm and like myself again, no longer hearing DeMario mocking me in my head. When I sat up, I saw Tiana standing in the parking lot a few feet away from my car. She stared at me as if she thought I was losing my mind. Hell, *I* thought I was losing my mind.

I roared up my Hellcat and peeled out of the parking lot. The faster I got out of there, the better.

Addict 3.0 – DeAngelo's Story

Chapter 3

I was on the stand the next day when I broke the collective hearts of my family. I hadn't heard my mother wail like that since they day I told her DeMario had been shot and killed.

That morning, Dear, what we called my mother, chewed me out on the steps of the courthouse for not calling her back yesterday. My head was too fucked up to talk to anyone, alive at least. I drove around the city after leaving Tiana's until I ended up at DeMario's grave ordering him to leave me alone then telling him how sorry I was that he was dead.

I still didn't say any of the things his ghost voice was pushing me to say while sitting in Tiana's parking lot. I told him that peace would come after I filet his murderer in court.

"So, your brother DeMario came to know the defendant because you introduced them."

"Yes," I answered.

Kim rose from her seat in the galley next to my empty one and rushed out the courtroom. She was truly the most innocent in the twisted love and lust pentagon she was inadvertently brought into when I introduced the murdering slut to her boyfriend, my twin brother. I knew she wondered how we both ended up involved with Destiny because she asked several times after DeMario's death. I was good at dodging answering her. It seemed that everyone was getting hurt by the truth.

"How did your relationships with the defendant evolve?"

I took a sip of water from the bottle in front of me. "There was a schedule, of sorts. We each met with her individually once per week, and then all together once per week. Sometimes if she asked, my brother and I together would get with her on another day.

Another gasp from my family.

"By '*get with* and *met'* you mean have sex?"

"Yes."

"How many men were involved with this schedule?" the A.D.A. asked. I hated what the answers to these questions were doing to my family, but I knew it was necessary if DeMario was going to have any type of justice.

"Three."

"Including or in addition to you and your brother?"

"Including."

A loud cry came from Dear and family members did what they could to try to console her. The judge banged his gavel and called for order. Dear continued to wail. Hearing her express her hurt in such a way nearly broke me as I wiped away my own tears. She was always a proud woman, never let others see her hurt and vulnerable. I didn't remember her crying at Suga's, her mother and my grandmother, funeral.

"Your Honor, I request we take a ten-minute recess for the witness and family of the victim to gather themselves before we continue," the A.D.A. suggested.

"I agree," the judge responded. "We'll take a ten-minute recess," he said before swinging his gavel.

I stayed in the witness box for a minute after my family filed out of the courtroom. I didn't want to go out there. If Dear managed to say anything to me, I knew she would curse me out and cut me off. That would be before my sister, youngest brother, cousins, aunts, and uncle all beat my ass with whatever time was left. Just when I decided to stay right where I was in the witness box for the duration of the recess to let everyone cool off, my only sister stuck her head in between the doors and looked straight at me.

"Come on," she told me. I could never tell her *no* and in that moment, I knew it would not be the first. As I left the box and walked between the prosecution and defense tables, the she-devil called out my name. I hesitated for a bit but kept walking.

"You know you miss me and what we had, DeAngelo."

"Destiny, no. You don't talk to him or anyone except us," I heard her lawyers scold her. I made eye contact with Andre and shook my head. Besides a couple of her clients who stuck out in the nearly all Black galley, he was the only person there to support her. She stopped communicating with her family long ago, so whoever they are, they may not have known she was on trial for murder. Or they knew and kept their distance like they did when they found out she was earning her money as a Dominatrix.

I followed my sister, Deidra, to where my family was down the hall from the courtroom. They were all to one side while I stood in front of them on the other side, like I was on the wrong side of a firing squad. I made eye contact with no one.

My uncle was the first to speak up. "I can only imagine the guilt you've been carrying around this entire time."

His words were not what I expected to hear. I looked at him and saw empathetic eyes.

"DeAngelo, why didn't you tell us? Is this why you haven't been around since DeMario's funeral?" Deidra asked. My eyes went to her, but I failed at expressing words.

"DeAngelo," Dear called.

"Ma'am."

"The burden you carry is too heavy for you alone."

I sobbed. "It's my fault, so I have to be the one to carry it," I said as I repeatedly jabbed a finger at my chest.

"Boy, no you don't," my uncle said as he charged towards me and embraced me. Next thing I knew, I was in the middle of a

Bealle family group hug. I cried like I had not let myself do since Kim called to tell me that DeMario attacked her and the she-devil and he was dead. Of course, Kim didn't know or realize that it was all a set up at the time.

When everyone pulled apart from the group hug, I looked at my mother. I mean, I really looked at her for the first time since DeMario died. She had aged some. There were wrinkles in the corners of her eyes that weren't there before. Her eyes looked weary like she'd been crying for months. Grief from losing DeMario and my distance had attributed to that. "I'm sorry, Dear."

I've finally admitted my guilt out loud. I've finally done what the ghost of my twin brother asked me to do. Well, at least one of the things he asked me to do.

Chapter 4

About a week after the trial and sentencing, I reached out to Tiana and she invited me over to her place. Sitting in her living room, I tried to explain to her what happened to me the last time I was over some weeks ago.

"Not only did you imagine me as your ex—"

"She's not my ex," I corrected.

"Call it whatever you want, but you were also seeing your dead brother."

"I was hearing him," I corrected her again. "We're identical twins, I see him whenever I look in the mirror. Always have." I think back on the old camcorder video of me and DeMario sitting on a small bathroom counter looking in the mirror and us pointing to our own reflection when asked where the other twin was.

"Did you love her?" Tiana asked me, bringing me back from when times were much, much simpler.

"What?"

"Did you love her?" she repeated.

"No. Hell naw! Only one of the three of us was dumb enough to fall in love with that hoe and I was not that fool."

"But you cared for her."

I released a hard sigh. "No." *What is she getting at?*

"You were messing around with her for years. Even you aren't that callous to not have at least cared for her."

I rolled my eyes at Tiana, not only because of how ridiculous she sounded but also because she sounded just like the ghost voice of my brother.

"It's okay if you cared for her and struggle reconciling what she did, DeAngelo. It would be understandable."

I let it slip who she sounded like.

"Look at me, DeAngelo." I slowly dragged my eyes up to hers. "I could be wrong, but I think the voice of your brother is really your conscience telling you everything you've been holding in from everyone, including yourself. What you haven't been willing to admit or accept."

I shook my head and turned away from her. "Look, I didn't come over here to be lectured. I just wanted to explain what happened and apologize again."

"And to talk to someone who isn't family and wouldn't judge you."

I shook my head and she chuckled.

"Fine. Don't admit it," she said while still laughing. "I just want you to realize that this is the first time in the few months we've been messing around where you came over here for something other than my cooking and sex."

I sigh again. She had me there.

"Uh huh," Tiana said with a cocky tone.

"Speaking of food and sex…" I said with a sly smile. "You gonna feed a brother or what?"

"I outta give you a bowl of cereal and a juice box for leaving me hanging last time."

I smacked my lips and leaned towards her in a joking way. "You act like you didn't call one of the gang of men your fine ass has in your phone, like I told you to."

Tiana gave me a pout. "I wanted you."

The seductive bratty tone she spoke in sent a current right to my dick. It started to come alive as I looked at her in nothing but a tank top and some panties. "You're saying them other ones can't fuck you right?" I asked.

"No. I'm saying the other ones don't make me want to obey…sir."

"Is that right?"

She bit her bottom lip and nodded. I noticed how she squeezed her thighs as she answered. She wanted me…bad. I was hoping that since court was over with, I would mentally be up for the task. "Well, since you've been such a good girl about all of this, how about I treat you with a spanking—"

"And some eating then fucking," she quickly interjected. I raised an eyebrow at her. "Sorry, sir," she said before giving me a sexy smile. I always loved how I could get her or any woman I messed around with to fall in line with just a look.

"How do you want me to spank you?" I asked her after a few moments of making her squirm.

"With your hand," she responded in an innocent tone.

I cupped her chin in my hand and leaned in close to her face. "Attention."

Tiana got off the couch and bent over the arm of it, putting her chest into the cushion she was just sitting on. I rose from the couch, placed a hand in the small of her back, and rubbed and squeezed her ass to warm it up. It had been a minute since I released my inner Dominant on anyone. This was just what I needed.

My hand smacked her ass, not hard, as starting too rough could have ended the play time before it got started. Based on her words earlier and her moans from my touch, Tiana needed this just as much as I did.

I increased the intensity of the spanks. "Is this what you want?"

"Harder, sir."

I gave her what she asked for. "Like this?"

"Yes," she panted. I gave her an even harder smack. "Yes, sir."

I found a rhythm, spanking her all around her tight round ass, hips, and the back of her thighs. Tiana moaned and her breath caught in her throat as I gave her what she asked for. I loved seeing her, any woman I was intimate with, this way. Totally relaxed, trusting me completely, and floating high on the attention I gave them.

I used to do this regularly with… *No. No.* I stopped the thought immediately. I was not going to allow myself to think of *her*. I was determined to stay in this moment with Tiana and not leave her hanging again.

I kept spanking Tiana until her body let me know she was at her limit; with Tiana, that was when she started sliding down the arm of the couch. I picked her up before she hit the carpet and carried her to her bedroom. Laying her down on her bed, she softly cooed, still floating on kink bliss. I spread and pushed her legs up and dined on her pussy like I was starving for her. I hadn't had any in a bit, so I guess I was.

Tiana grinded and rotated her pussy on my face as I licked and sucked on her flesh. Her moans were the sexiest I've ever head. Soft. Airy. Soprano. Nothing like the loud aggressive moans of … *Dammit, no.* I didn't understand why I couldn't keep that murderer out of my mind. I refocused on the task at hand. Tiana.

After increasing the speed of my tongue flicks on her clit, her body started shaking, results of the first of several orgasms I planned to give her. Tiana moaned softly and incoherently, while I continued eating her, feeling her tremble in her most precious space. My licks and suckles were gentler at this point, aware of how sensitive her clitoris was now that she came.

I loved the way she purred like a kitten being scratched the right way. When her breathing calmed, I began to pick up the pace of my tongue again and the intensity of my sucks. I was determined to pop her off one more time before putting my dick into her. It was both for her pleasure and my ego. Tiana easily got into rolling orgasms after her second or third orgasm. If I get the first two out the way with oral, she would be quaking and cumming on my dick damn near nonstop once I got inside of her.

I felt the covers being pulled on while I focused on her. She was fisting the bedding, getting close to her second nut. Her back arched off the bed and her legs tightened around my head. I licked her harder until she came again. Her shakes were so intense I thought she was going to snap my neck on some Mortal Kombat type shit. I wanted to slide into her as she was cumming but the vice grip hold her legs had on my head prevented that.

When her thighs loosened their grip, I stood up and in quick movements, pulled her body down to the edge of the bed, dropped my pants, put on a condom, and rammed into her. A shiver ran through my body once I was inside of her. I was going to have to focus to not pop off too soon. Damn, it felt good to be inside a tight pussy again. I wished I could go in raw like I did with…*no! Fuck! I almost did it again.*

I shook my head and refocused, again. Pulling almost all the way out of Tiana, I paused for a beat then rammed into her again. Her hands gripped my arms to brace herself as I did it. This time, I didn't stop and kept fucking her fast and hard.

Tiana laid beneath me with her mouth slacked like she wanted to moan but couldn't find her voice or breath. I gave her cheek a light slap and she inhaled deep, coming back to earth. She caught her breath while I grabbed one of her bouncing tits, squeezing and fondling it.

"Fuck," she moaned.

I felt her pussy walls tighten around my dick and it encouraged me to dig deeper into her. I did and placed a hand around her neck. Closing my eyes, I let the good feeling take over me and not before long, both my hands were around her neck. I could see her in my mind, but it was not the actual her that was under me in the moment.

Her.

In my mind's eyes, I could see her big titties bouncing from my thrusts. As much as I didn't want to think about that slut,

I was too far gone to stop my thoughts or this nut. I could even hear her moans. Loud. Erotic. Animalistic.

She was such a good slut. The best.

I pounded into her harder, like I was a tormented beast. Tormented by my lust for her and my desire to see her dead. I wanted to fuck her, kill her, and revive her just to fuck and kill her all over again. Keep doing it until I felt satisfied, which I probably never would. Just an endless loop of lust and death, death and lust.

I could feel my own orgasm rising, rising so slow that it was almost painful. Sweat beaded and ran down my forehead as, in my mind, I continued to pound into the woman I had every reason to hate, who I had been pretending to hate. Truth was, I hated myself for not being able to hate her.

In the exact moment I came to that realization, my orgasm moved through and out of me like a thunderbolt.

"Shit, Destiny," I growled as I released.

Immediately, I realized my mistake. I fucked up bad. I was never one to play around with other people's feelings, so I didn't bother trying to fake like I was saying something else. There wasn't a way to spin it no way.

With my eyes still closed, I pulled out of Tiana, who I noticed had gone dead silent and still. "I'm sorry," I said. I was.

"You were thinking about her, the woman that killed your twin brother," she said. I didn't know if my intentional lack of eye contact amplified her irritated tone or not, but I had never heard her sound so angry, at least not at me. "The woman whose name you said you would never speak again. You were fucking her instead of me."

This time my eyes went to hers. If looks could have killed, I would've been with DeMario instantly. "I said I was sorry."

"Admit it!"

I released a heavy sigh and headed towards her bathroom to removed and dispose of the condom. Standing in there, I wished I had grabbed my pants and briefs. It wasn't going to be comfortable facing Tiana again. I took my time washing up in hopes she would calm down some before heading back into her bedroom. "Look, I don't know what you want me to say," I told her.

"I want you to admit that you were fantasizing about Destiny while you were fucking me. Admit that you care for her."

I started putting my clothes on. "Yes! Yes, she was in my head while I was fucking you. Yes, I cared for her and don't know what to do with that when all I want to do is hate her!"

"Say her name," Tiana said.

"I already did. That's why we're having this conversation."

"That wasn't intentional."

I tried to blow her off again, but she still demanded that I say the name of the woman who had me in more ways than one, more ways than I realized until now. "Destiny! Fine! There, I said it. I was imagining I was fucking Destiny while I was fucking you. Are you happy now?"

"Almost." She stood in front of me, naked, spine straight. Her body language said she was on the defensive. "Either work out your feelings for her or don't bother coming back here again."

I nodded. I couldn't do anything but respect that. I'm grateful she didn't outright cuss me out for saying another woman's name. I left her place and headed to where my brother was buried to ask him for forgiveness for not hating the person who robbed him of happiness in the last weeks of his life before taking said life.

Addict 3.0 – DeAngelo's Story

Chapter 5

I was back at work after taking time off for the trial, plus an additional three weeks to get my head together. I didn't realize how much I missed being in the kitchen cooking up some of New Orleans' finest dishes. It felt good to get back to myself and putting the events and revelations of the past few months behind me, or so I thought.

A hostess walked into the kitchen saying there was a man at the door asking for me and that he had been by a couple of times while I was out. I frowned at her because anyone who knew me knew not to come looking for me at my job. More importantly, anyone that needed to get in contact with me knew how to do so.

I told her I would be up there in a minute and continued the dish I was making before handing it off to a line cook to finish and plate. I walked to the front of the restaurant and felt a pit in my stomach when I saw Andre standing there. He reminded me of everything I lost and hated about myself. I walked by him without a word, and he followed me outside, beyond the outdoor seating area, almost to the parking lot. Coming to an abrupt stop, I turned to face him and asked him what the fuck he wanted. My sharp tone gave him pause and he took a few seconds to recover.

"I've been put on probation from seeing Destiny for a while."

Initially, I gave him a blank stare then realized I was going to have to say what was going through my head. "Man, what the fuck does that have to do with me?"

"Have you been up to see her yet?"

What the hell? "No," I said with a flat tone.

"When do you think you are going?"

"Wh...why would I go up there, Andre? DeMario was my brother. My *twin* brother," I said while slapping the back of one hand into the palm of the other between the last three words. He looked at me like he was confused. *How was this dumbass an EMT?*

"Look Andre, I'm going to tell you like I told her the last time we talked before she killed my brother. Bros before hoes. Even in death. I've had to reconcile a lot of shit, but I will never disrespect the memory of my brother by going to visit the person that put him in the ground."

"I can't get to her, so I thought—"

"You thought wrong," I interrupted. "Stop fucking thinking because all of that shit is fucked up when it comes to Destiny. While you're at it, don't come up here again. I changed my number because of shit with her. I don't want to have to change jobs because of her too. Leave me alone and out of whatever twisted shit you got going on with Destiny." I started walking off to leave him in the parking lot.

"You didn't mind being all up in my shit with Destiny before," Andre snapped.

I stopped. He was right, I could give him that and told him so. "That was a mistake of mine. A mistake I will have to live with for the rest of my life. You do...whatever it is you do." I turned and went back to work. *The nerve of him. Crazy ass bastard.*

I thought the shit with Destiny was over with. I reconciled the fact that I cared for her against what she did. You know, hate the sin but not the sinner Gandhi type of deal. Here this dude was trying to bring his personal Destiny drama up to my job. *What the fuck! Why couldn't this mess be behind me already?*

Addict 3.0 – DeAngelo's Story

Chapter 6

Months went by without incident. I hadn't hit Tiana up since the last time I saw her. Even though I was in a better place with everything, I figured it was best to leave things where they were with her. In fact, I blocked and deleted the numbers to my other jump offs too. I had to take more time to take care of myself emotionally and I couldn't see myself doing it while being fuck buddies with others.

Interesting how different women look to you when you aren't trying to fuck them as soon as possible.

Shit in my life had been pretty cool and benign until one night I noticed an old school Chevy following me one night after work. I knew plenty of people with older Chevy's but only one person who kept a pristine white with black stripe Chevy Nova.

Andre.

Not even Destiny knew where I lived, and he wasn't about to learn either. Lakeview Grocery was coming up soon, just past where I would have normally turned at. I figured its parking lot was an open and public enough space to talk or fight, depending on what his intentions were. My guess was fight since he was stalking me. I pulled in and so did Andre. Andre hung back at the end of the lane as I searched for a good spot to park. I went to pull into a parking spot that was close enough to the store to be seen on camera but far enough away from the ears of shoppers being able to hear us if we weren't yelling. Only, I didn't make it into the parking spot as planned.

Andre must have floored his gas pedal just as I was starting to turn because his front end went into my driver's side near the back.

"What the fuck!" I yelled when I realized what was happening. He pushed the back end of my car into a cart chorale, making my front end go into the side of the car on the other side of the parking spot. I guess his anger towards me was greater than his love for his classic car. No way in hell I would have done that with my Hellcat! My Hellcat!

This couldn't possibly be over Destiny after all this time, but deep down I knew it was. Sex with Destiny was good. It was great. She didn't have a lot of the inhibitions other women had, but great sex wasn't worth all this though. It for damn sure wasn't worth either one of our cars or a damn criminal record.

"Have you lost your motherfucking mind!" I yelled at him since both our windows were down. He was looking at me while appearing to struggle to get something from under his seat. My gut told me I had underestimated him. This wasn't going to be a talk or a fist fight like I thought before. He came to kill me, and he was most likely reaching for a gun. Andre would had been able to get a new one since he wasn't the one to commit a crime when Destiny used his gun to kill DeMario. Moving as fast as I could, I undid my seatbelt, climbed over to the passenger seat, and tried to open the door. It wouldn't budge. It must had gotten jammed from him pushing me into and along the cart chorale.

Shit.

I turned back to look, and he was still struggling. My fingers clumsily found the button to let down the window and because I was in a hurry, it felt like it was moving slower than usual. Andre raised his arm just as the window got all the way open. I hightailed it out of my car window headfirst, but not before he managed to get a couple shots off. The first one missed me, but the second shot hit me in the leg.

I fell hard onto the pavement and held my leg just above where the bullet went into my calf.

Andre yelled like a wild animal. "Everything was perfect before you showed up! Then you just had to bring your brother along!"

Looking under my car, I could see his car moving but I didn't see his feet, which meant he hadn't gotten out of his car yet. I knew if I was going to make it out alive, I needed to move, but running on my shot leg wasn't an option. I army crawled as fast as I could to the back side of the car facing the space I was in. By the time I got there, Andre was out of his car.

Sitting by the back passenger tire of the car I was hiding behind, which was opposite of where Andre stood, I contemplated my next moves while he was still ranting on about how I ruined his life and everything he thought he and Destiny had. I thought about running into the store, but he could have shot me in the back or killed others just to get to me. Neither one was acceptable for me.

I was going to have to fight him. Or find a way to hold him off until NOPD showed up. I didn't want to do it because he could've killed me in the process. As much as I missed DeMario, I wasn't ready to be with my brother again. I also didn't want my death to have anything to do with Destiny.

"She was mine!" Andre yelled hysterically.

Is he drunk, crying, or both?

"You knew she had someone else, but you couldn't help yourself. Guess what DeAngelo! That makes you the whore, not her!"

The gun went off again and I heard a woman scream the name 'Robert' over and over again.

"Robert?" Andre said like he was confused. "I thought that was the girlfriend stealing asshole named DeAngelo. My fault."

That was what I feared as much as my own death. I had never been a religious person, but I closed my eyes and asked whoever was up there to let me and everyone else that had nothing to do with this craziness get out of this alive, including Robert.

I looked under the car and saw Andre's shoes by the trunk of his car. The air was still, and the only sounds were my racing heart, Andre's ranting, a woman crying, and the passing traffic.

"Where the fuck are you DeAngelo?" he yelled as I made my way around the back and side of the car I had been hiding behind. "You were bold enough to try to take the woman I love away from me in front of my face but can't face me to pay the consequences of it! What kind of shit is that?"

I got close enough to see the back of his head. Andre turned a bit to the side, and I watched him bring a bottle of Bou Jae vodka up to his mouth. *I was right about the drinking. Dude was deep in his feelings because that was Destiny's favorite brand of vodka.* I watched enough of my drunk family members to know that alcohol and crazy did not mix well at all.

I moved as close to him as I could while still staying hidden. I was now by his back driver-side tire. My leg was hurting bad at this point, but I couldn't focus on that in the moment. I was just grateful that it didn't seem to be bleeding much. Andre was still ranting and raving while I took a few deep breaths to gather myself. Counting to three in my head, I got ready.

1. 2. 3.

I charged at him as hard and fast as I could on a bum leg. Thankfully, he didn't hear me coming until I was already on him. He turned around, surprised to see me so close to him and without enough time to raise his gun to get another shot off at me. I tackled him to the unforgiving blacktop of the parking lot. With my hands under his body, they were scraped against the pavement, but I was sure I heard the gun fall and hit the ground. Still, I didn't want to chance him being able to pop off another round, whether at me or another innocent person.

I pulled my hands up from under him and began punching his face. In between punches, I took the chance to look at his hands. They were empty, but I had no idea where the gun was. Wherever it was, I had to keep him from getting to it, so I kept hitting him as hard as I could while trying to block out my own pain. My right fist was screaming for me to stop but I couldn't. My life depended on it.

Andre's face was bleeding from his nose and mouth. He reached up, grabbed the collar of my shirt, and yanked me down to him all while bringing his head up to meet mine.

The headbutt was powerful. I was stunned and fell off him. The pain to my nose was immediate and sharp. I felt blood running out and over my lips. Fighting to regain my focus, I saw Andre doing the same while looking for the gun. I started looking for it too, out of desperation to find it and get to it before he did.

I spotted the gun just under a cart in the chorale and headed towards it. The only problem was that Andre spotted it at the same time I did. He tried to push me out the way when we reached the opening of the chorale, but I managed to grab his shirt and pull him back. I went for the gun. I almost got to it, but Andre was just as determined to kill me as I was determined to live. He kicked the back of my knee and put his arm around my neck. Andre had me in a choke hold. The fight of my life turned into a wrestling main event. One that seemed to be rigged for me to lose.

As I tried to pull his arm lose to get the air I was in dire need of and failing to get, all I could think about was how I never found the love that I told Destiny everyone wanted. The love my dead twin brother found with Kim but fucked up. The kind that Andre wanted to have with Destiny.

I began losing consciousness and my next thought was my mother having to bury another of her sons. Two of her four kids would leave this earth early and violently while not leaving a grandchild or anything for her or the world. Selfish in every way, DeMario and I.

I felt my body collapse to the ground, not completely out of it but in urgent need of air. Coughing and gasping for a breath, I couldn't do anything to stop Andre from getting to the gun. He could have killed me if he kept me in that chokehold a bit longer. Knowing his crazy ass, he wanted the pleasure of taking me out the same way Destiny took out DeMario.

My last breath was about to not be a full breath and there was nothing I could do about it. Andre stood over me pointing the gun at my chest as I still strained to give my body oxygen.

"Everything that was important to me," he said with heavy pants and blood dripping from his face, "everything I loved and could have had is gone. All. Because. Of. You. My life with Destiny would be perfect right now if you had never come around. Now she won't even see me! Me!" He pounded on his chest. "The only one who loved her!"

He straightened his arm, ready to shoot. There were multiple gunshots. Too many too fast to be from one pistol. None of the bullets seemed to be hitting me, unless my adrenaline was so high that I couldn't feel shit. I covered my head like it was supposed to give me some form of protection while laying out in the open.

When the bullets stopped flying, I uncurled from the ball I was in and checked my body over with my hands. *Only one bullet hole still, I think.*

Lifting my head, I saw Andre laying at my feet motionless.

"Stay down!" was yelled at me from behind where I laid. It wasn't until then when I registered the sound of several footsteps behind me. I laid flat on the ground as I didn't want to be the latest trending topic on social media.

"Turn over!"

"You shot the man with the gun. I didn't do anything!"

"Turn over and put your hands behind your back!" I did as instructed and immediately there were multiple hands on me, one set holding me down at my shoulders and the other placing cuffs on me.

"I told y'all that I didn't do anything! You saw the other man with the gun. He was trying to kill me!"

"Calm down. You're not under arrest unless you give us a reason to arrest you. This is just to safely move you out of the crime scene. Don't resist."

I laid there breathing hard, doing my best to not fight against them. I was well aware of the fact that the smallest of movements on my part could be seen as resisting from a Black man, especially a dark-skinned man involved in a shooting incident, nonetheless.

"We're going to pull you up," an officer said to me.

"I was shot in my leg."

"By us or the other guy?"

"Andre. The other guy," I answered.

"Alright, when we stand you up, raise the leg injured and we'll carry you to a safe spot."

I nodded my head and I heard a nearby officer radio for medics. In one swift move, the officers lifted me up by my arms that were handcuffed behind my back, then carried me several feet away. I looked around and saw Robert laying on the pavement. They sat me down on a parking block on the edge of the lot.

"Do you know the other man that was shot?" This was the first time I was able to look at the officers talking to me. I could barely see their eyes through their face shields due to the glare from the streetlights. They were in full tactical gear like they were ready for war or a riot.

"No. He was a passerby. There was a female with him. She is out here somewhere. Is he alive?"

"I don't know, but my colleagues will figure that out. You know what started the incident?"

"Yeah, but I have to go back a few months to give you the whole story."

The officer took out a notebook and pen. I sighed, both because it was a heavy story and how close I came to death. But thinking on it, I did die. Not in the physical sense obviously, but a part of me did.

DeMario died.

Andre died.

The part of me that believed in love overcoming all died.

All three deaths were the result of being an addict of the wrong piece of pussy. In the end, it wasn't worth all the damage it caused.

A Note from the Author:

At the end of Addict, Andre was the person I felt sorry for the most, because he just LOVED Destiny. After being bullied by some readers into writing the guy's stories (that is my story and I'm sticking to it), DeAngelo is most certainly the one who has my deepest sympathies.

Writing DeAngelo's story, I was relieved to no longer be living in Andre's head, but feeling DeAngelo's broken heart and his grief was something different entirely. Grief hits us in different ways, especially when you aren't trying to deal with the grief, and everything associate with what brought that grief on. My heart broke for DeAngelo. He wasn't in love with Destiny but the part of him that cared for her and didn't want to see her hurt battled greatly with wanting to see her pay for killing DeMario.

Here is a little BTS on this book. This is the one of the four books in the Addict Series that I struggled to write the most. Initially, the only antagonist I had for DeAngelo was his grief, but the story would have ended two chapters earlier and this was already going to be a short book, but not *that* short. I had to go back to Andre's story to change his final scene because I initially had him committing suicide in the car directly after his last prison visit attempt with Destiny. Yup! I had to rewrite that so that he could go after DeAngelo. The last chapter of Andre's book and the last chapter of DeAngelo's book happen on the same day.

I almost…almost wrote an additional book that brough DeAngelo together with the characters of my Love Lost Series, by having him move to Detroit to open his own restaurant for a fresh start and meeting and falling for JaQuese, Jaylen and Alise's oldest daughter. Jaylen wasn't going to like him, DeAngelo was going to introduce Quese to BDSM, Quese was going to talk to Alise about it and Jaylen found out about it and wanted to kill DeAngelo (as any father would), Otis was going to have to step in, and of course, at least one person was going to have to die at some point. Don't look at me (this page) like that. If you have been with me since Love Lost, you know someone is going to die.

But I changed my mind on writing that one. Anyway…

The final book of the Addict Series, Addict 4.0 – DeMario's Story, is next. In it, the question of why DeMario got involved with Destiny in the first place will finally be answered.

Thanks for coming on this ride with me.

Porsha Deun

Thank you for reading my book! I feel honored, truly.

Did you enjoy Addict 3.0 – DeAngelo's Story? Be sure to leave a review on your favorite online book retailer, Goodreads, Bookbub, or my Facebook Page!

You can preview and purchase the rest of my books on my website, as well as with your favorite online book retailer! Be sure to sign up for my mailing list while you are on my website. My Love Bugs get cover reveals at least a month before the public, as well as surprises and giveaways. www.porshadeun.com.

Love Lost Series
Love Lost
Love Lost Forever
Love Lost Revenge

Addict Series
Addict – A Fatal Attraction Story
Addict 2.0 – Andre's Story
Addict 3.0 – DeAngelo's Story
Addict 4.0 – DeMario's Story (August 2021)

Standalones
Intoxic (October 2021)

Children's Book
Princesses Can Do Anything!

CPSIA information can be obtained
at www.ICGtesting.com
Printed in the USA
BVHW071737260721
612868BV00006B/359